POKÉMON

DESTINY DEOXYS

A film adaptation by Tracey West

SCHOLASTIC INC.

New York   Toronto   London   Auckland   Sydney

Mexico City   New Delhi   Hong Kong   Buenos Aires

ISBN 0-439-74145-9

12 11 10 9 8 7 6 5 4 3 2 1   5 6 7 8 9/0

Printed in the U.S.A.
First printing, March 2005

PROLOGUE

A freezing wind blew across the ice field. Professor Lund focused his binoculars. Through the lens, he could see Sealeo and Walrein sliding on the ice. The fat in their round, blue bodies protected them from the bitter cold.

Behind the professor, his crew was busy pitching tents and setting up equipment. Their ship was anchored in the water nearby. They had traveled north to study Pokémon that live in the Earth's coldest regions. He had been preparing for the trip for years. So far, everything was going smoothly. Only one thing worried him.

Lund lowered his binoculars. Next to him, his assistant, Yuko, was focused on a figure on the ice. Looking down, Lund saw his five-year-old son, Tory, walking away from the camp. The boy moved slowly toward the Sealeo.

Lund smiled. Maybe he should not have been worried about bringing Tory after all. Yes, Tory was young to come on a trip like this. But his son was used to the lab and the machines. He was curious about Pokémon, just like his father. He would be fine.

Then something else caught Lund's eye. A brilliant, glowing light appeared over the horizon. The reddish-gold colors seemed to pulse with light as they brightened the dark sky.

"An aurora!" Lund cried. He knew the phenomenon—a spectacular light show created by electric energy—was common in the North, but he had never seen one before. It was beautiful.

Suddenly, meteors streaked down across the aurora, aimed right at their camp. As the meteors sped by, a gust of wind kicked up. Lund watched helplessly as the wind picked up Tory and deposited him in the middle of the Sealeo.

"Tory!" Lund cried.

The Pokémon cried out in alarm as Tory landed among them. Frightened, they charged Tory, batting him around with their flat noses. Lund ran between them and picked up his son. Tory's eyes were closed.

"You're okay. I've got you," Lund said reassuringly.

Lund had to get Tory back to the ship, but a thick haze had formed across the ice. He would have to make his way carefully.

Then he stopped in his tracks.

The haze parted, and Lund saw a Pokémon standing there. It did not look like any Pokémon he had ever seen before. Its smooth, blue face had two vacant, black eyes, but no nose or mouth. Its body was red, and its long legs ended in points. It had long arms and large hands.

Lund watched, amazed, as the Pokémon picked up a black chunk of the meteor. A smooth, gold crystal, shaped like an egg, was embedded inside it. The Pokémon sadly looked at the crystal.

"It's a Pokémon from outer space," whispered Lund.

Without warning, a green, dragonlike Pokémon flew down from the sky. Fear shot through Lund's body. Fierce Rayquaza was one of the most powerful and dangerous Pokémon alive.

Rayquaza shot a Hyper Beam at the strange Pokémon. The powerful light beam blasted off the Pokémon's arm—but another one quickly grew in its place.

Lund did not wait to see the rest of the battle. He ran back to the ship, having grabbed Tory.

"Let's go!" he cried. "It's too dangerous!"

On the ice field, Rayquaza blasted the strange Pokémon with another Hyper Beam. This time, the attack hit the Pokémon in the center of its body. There was a sickening scream as pieces of the Pokémon's body scattered across the ice field. All that was left of it was a glowing crystal—just like the one in the meteor—that began to sink into the ocean.

The professor loaded Tory, Yuko, and his crew into a helicopter. As they flew away, a claw on the bottom of the helicopter grabbed the meteor with the egg-shaped crystal in it.

"Rayquaza is furious," Lund told Yuko. "Another Pokémon crossing into its territory has obviously threatened it."

Beside him, Tory continued to shiver with fear.

Four years later . . .

Professor Lund named the Pokémon from outer space Deoxys. He had spent four years studying the crystal. Over that time, he and Yuko developed a theory.

"The crystal is like the heart of Deoxys," Lund explained. "If we charge the crystal with enough energy, we can regenerate Deoxys to its complete form. We can bring it back to life."

Lund and Yuko set up a special underground lab to study the crystal. They encased it in a capsule and attached the capsule to a laser generator. Lund aimed a laser beam at the crystal.

"This has got to work," Lund said.

The laser beam hit the crystal. Immediately, the crystal began to glow and pulse, as though it were going to change form.

The machines in the lab began to spark and shake.

"It's too much power!" Lund yelled.

The machines stopped. The crystal returned to its original shape.

Lund sighed. "We will just have to keep trying."

But the experiment hadn't failed completely. Far away, in the cold North, another Pokémon sensed the energy of the crystal. The icy water began to bubble, and then something burst through the ice, restored to its original form . . .

Deoxys!

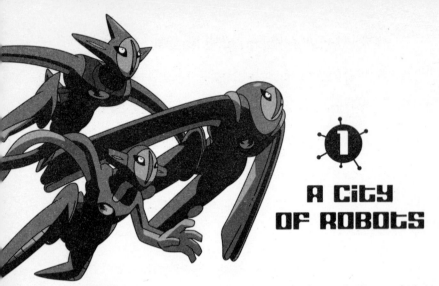

1

A CITY OF ROBOTS

Ash Ketchum stared out the window of the monorail as the sleek train raced across the track high in the air. Ash's yellow Electric Pokémon, Pikachu, stood by his side. A wide river flowed below them, and through the window, Ash saw Larousse City sitting on a sandy island in the middle of the river.

The island was small, but crowded with buildings and people. Large windmills circled the island. A very tall tower rose up in the center of the island, surrounded by laboratories, houses, parks, and Pokémon Centers.

Ash pointed to the tower. "That must be the Battle Tower, Pikachu," he said.

"Pika! Pika!" Pikachu said happily.

Ash's friend Brock stepped up beside him. The dark-haired boy wore a green vest. "The Battle Tower in Larousse City is one of the most famous in the world," Brock remarked.

"That's because it's so technologically advanced," Ash's friend Max piped up. The young boy adjusted the glasses on his face. "Just about everything in Larousse City is controlled by robots."

Max's sister, May, joined them. "Cool!" she said, her eyes shining with excitement. "Do you think we'll get to meet one?"

Just then, the monorail glided to a smooth stop. The door in front of Ash and his friends opened, and they stepped out onto the platform. A security robot stood there ready to greet them.

"Welcome, you are now in Larousse City," the robot said.

A flash of light shot from the robot. Seconds later, plastic cards slid out of a slot on the robot's body. Ash grabbed them. Each card had a photo of Ash and his friends.

"These will serve as your passports," the robot informed them. "While in Larousse City, keep them with you at all times. Your passports can be used for shopping and other needs."

May looked at her picture. Her face had a silly, surprised look on it, and her brown hair was sticking up in the air.

"Don't think I'll be sending *this* one home," May muttered.

"So I wonder which way to go to the Battle Tower," Ash said.

Ash and Pikachu ran through the door of the monorail station. Suddenly, Ash felt the ground move beneath him. He looked down. He and Pikachu had stepped on to a moving sidewalk!

"HELP!" cried Ash.

"Hey Ash! Quit messing around!" May yelled.

Ash and Pikachu turned around. They tried to run back to Brock, Max, and May, but the sidewalk kept pulling them forward.

"Dude, you're swimming *upstream*!"

Ash turned toward the voice. A boy around his age was heading toward him on a moving sidewalk coming from the opposite direction. The serious-looking boy wore a formal-looking suit. He was accompanied by two young twin girls and another boy his age.

The boy in the suit threw a Poké Ball. "Help him out Blaziken, okay?" Rafe asked.

A tall, imposing Pokémon with red feathers on its body popped out of the ball. It grabbed onto Ash and Pikachu with its strong arms and lifted them onto the sidewalk next to the boy.

"Hey thanks a lot!" Ash said, a little shaken. He and Pikachu started to run back toward their friends.

"I just couldn't continue watching you look like a fool," the boy said.

Ash turned around. "What?" He was grateful to the boy for helping him, but he didn't like being called a fool.

"If you and your friends are headed for the Battle Tower, you should try going this way," the boy said.

Soon all of the friends were riding on the moving sidewalk.

"My names Ash from Pallet Town! How would you like to battle with me?" he asked.

The two little girls looked up at the boy in the suit. One girl said, "Watch out, my brother Rafe's really strong!"

"Blaziken, too!" said the other.

"I'd love to have a battle with you Ash. Let's get together at the Battle Tower, okay?" answered Rafe.

As they got closer to the Battle Tower, the sidewalk lanes became more complicated, crisscrossing each other. A pretty girl with glasses, and a notebook computer under her arm, zipped up next to them in another lane.

"So we're finally going to settle this today right, Rafe," she said.

Rafe didn't have a chance to answer, because Brock started running toward the girl. "Ah! Hello my bespectacled beauty! I'm Brock."

Max pulled Brock back by his shirt. "Stop!" he said.

The boy next to Rafe turned to May. "Well I guess you could say that your friend here has really *fallen* for Rebecca, huh! She's a good Metagross Trainer. She likes to use her laptop for strategy."

"So, my name is Sid. Blastoise is *my* partner," the boy said.

May smiled. "Hi! I'm May, and this is my brother, Max."

Sid looked into May's eyes. "Hey. You're kind of cute."

May's smile turned to a frown. "*Kind of*?"

"Look! The Battle Tower!" called Audrey.

"Look Pikachu! It's right there!" hollered Ash. "I can't wait!"

The moving sidewalk carried them to the entrance of the Battle Tower. In front of them, a number of escalators ran up and down in different directions. Ash and Pikachu ran to the nearest escalator.

"I'll be back as soon as I'm registered!" Ash called to his friends.

"Okay, then we'll head to the stands," answered Max.

But Ash hadn't looked at the signs. "Uh oh, now where are we?" Ash said to himself.

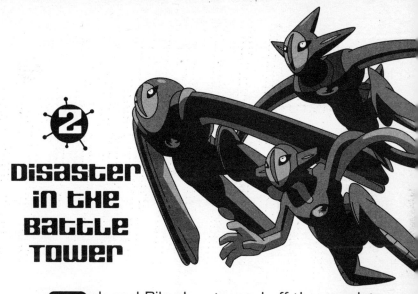

2
Disaster in the Battle Tower

Ash and Pikachu stepped off the escalator, confused. The room in front of them looked like some kind of library. But there was nobody in the room except a young boy sitting at a table and reading a book—Professor Lund's son, Tory. Ash walked up to him.

"Excuse me," he said.

Tory looked up from his book. When he saw Pikachu, he screamed in surprise and stumbled backward off of his chair.

"Hold on! What are you running away for?" Ash asked.

Tory didn't say a word. He quickly left the library.

"Wait! Hold up!" Ash called as he ran after Tory.

In the hallway, Ash stopped to catch his breath and tried again. "Hi! We're on our way to a battle but we don't know how to get there. So we're kind of lost . . ."

Tory took off again before Ash could finish. Luckily there was a big, burly man in a uniform coming down the hall.

"Are you ready for your battle?" the battle official asked. "Right this way gentlemen!" he said. He grabbed Ash with one arm and Tory with the other and rushed them down the hall.

"But you don't understand!" Tory yelled.

"If you hurry up, you two might just make it," the official said. He pushed the boys onto another moving sidewalk. Pikachu jumped on behind them.

The sidewalk whisked them under an entrance

gate as a robot's voice announced, "Passports confirmed. Two youth-level participants entered successfully."

"Great! And just in time!" Ash cheered.

"*Pika!*" Pikachu cheered with him.

But next to them, Tory looked pale and terrified.

The moving sidewalk deposited them in a small blue room that looked like a round box. The voice of the battle announcer reverberated through the tower.

"Our first match will be an Official Battle Tower Tag Team event! Remember to cheer for your favorites!"

The box went rising upward, carrying Ash, Tory, and Pikachu like some kind of elevator. The box stopped in a huge battle stadium. Fans cheered in the stands around the battle arena.

Tory looked like he was going to faint.

But Ash was too excited to notice. He waved at the crowd.

The announcer's voice rang out again. "We have

Ash Ketchum in the blue corner, a Trainer all the way from Pallet Town, and his tag partner, Tory, a local Trainer!"

Across the arena, a red box rose up through the floor. Rafe and Sid were inside.

"And in the red corner, we have two Trainers from South City, Rafe and Sid!"

Rafe and Sid waved at the crowd. Then Rafe turned to Ash.

"Hey Ash, you sure didn't waste any time," he said.

"Of course not. I couldn't wait to beat you," Ash said firmly.

"The basic rule in all tag battles is teamwork," the announcer said. "Each Trainer uses a single Pokémon and works with his teammate. And now Trainers, bring out your Pokémon!"

A battlefield rose up between the Trainer boxes. The top of the field was curved, like a small hill. If a

Pokémon got pushed off of the battlefield, it would fall to the arena below.

Rafe and Sid threw out their Poké Balls. Rafe's Blaziken and Sid's Blastoise burst out. Blastoise had a big, hard shell with two powerful water cannons sticking out from either side.

"Pikachu! I choose you!" Ash cried. He turned to Tory. "What Pokémon are you going to use?"

"I don't have any Pokémon," Tory said.

Ash was shocked. "But . . . "

"I was trying to tell you," Tory said. "I'm not a Trainer. I can't battle!"

Ash could have called off the battle, but he didn't want to back down. "This could be my only chance to battle Rafe," he said. "I'll loan you one of my Pokémon. What do you say?"

"But—" Tory protested.

Ash didn't listen. He handed Tory a Poké Ball.

"Don't let me down, Tory!" he said.

Tory sighed. "Well if I have to!"

Tory threw the ball, and Torkoal appeared. Ash's Fire Pokémon looked like an orange turtle with a hard shell. Smoke poured from Torkoal's nostrils.

"Looks like we have our Pokémon! Ready for battle? Because here we go!" the announcer yelled.

Blaziken made the first move. It charged at Pikachu with a Blaze Kick attack.

"Dodge Pikachu!" Ash yelled.

Pikachu quickly moved to the side, missing Blaziken's powerful leg.

"Go Blastoise, Hydro Pump!" Sid cried.

Blastoise shot powerful blasts of water from its water cannons, aimed at Pikachu. The little Pokémon dodged out of the way again.

Ash turned to Tory. "You have to tell Torkoal to do something!"

"But I don't know what to tell it!" Tory wailed.

Tory missed his turn. Sid ordered Blastoise to use Rapid Spin. The force of the attack sent Torkoal reeling.

The fight reminded Tory of Sealeo and Walrein charging at him when he was only five years old. He suddenly froze with fear.

"Pikachu, use Thunderbolt! Cover Torkoal!" Ash yelled.

Sid answered back. "Blastoise, Skull Bash! Go!"

Blastoise grunted. It lowered its head and collided into Pikachu with its thick head. Pikachu couldn't dodge the attack this time. The Electric Pokémon went flying and landed on top of Torkoal.

Tory still couldn't move. Ash shook his head in frustration.

"Tory, don't worry. I'll take care of it!" he said. "Flamethrower, Torkoal. Go!"

But Torkoal was confused. It wasn't expecting to get orders from Ash. It launched a burning hot flame—right at Pikachu!

Across the battlefield, Rafe laughed. "How embarrassing," he said.

"So Rafe, want to finish this one up?" Sid asked.

Rafe grinned. "Let's go Blaziken, Overheat!"

Blaziken charged toward Pikachu and Torkoal and hit them both with a powerful punch. The two Pokémon went flying up into the air, then landed with a crash. They didn't move.

"And that's it," said the announcer. "Pikachu and Torkoal are unable to battle! Rafe and Sid are the winners!"

3
STRANGE LIGHTS IN THE GARDEN

Both Pokémon opened their eyes and staggered to their feet. Ash led them back to the blue Trainer box, where Tory waited, still looking stunned. Automatically, the box sank back down to the Trainers' waiting area.

Professor Lund and Yuko ran through the door.

"Tory! We just watched your Pokémon battle. I'm incredibly proud!" Lund cried.

Tory snapped out of his daze. "Don't be. It was all an accident," Tory explained. "It wasn't supposed to happen."

Tory handed the Poké Ball back to Ash. Then he walked away. Tory's father followed him. Ash started to run after Tory, but Brock, Max, and May entered the room.

Yuko stepped forward. "We apologize for the mix-up with your battle. Tory is completely afraid of Pokémon," she said. "About four years ago, he had a very traumatic experience and it left him terrified of them. Sadly, he still hasn't managed to get over those fears."

Now Ash understood what had happened on the battlefield. "Wow!" he said. "I shouldn't have pushed him so hard."

Yuko frowned. "Underneath it all I think he loves them. All he really needs is the chance to get to know them."

That sounded like another challenge to Ash. "Then I'll give him that chance," he said. "All he needs now is to become friends with me and Pikachu. Right, Pikachu?" Ash asked.

"Pika! Pika!" Pikachu agreed.

Max, May, and Brock all agreed to help. Yuko thanked them, and they all split up to find Tory.

Ash and Pikachu stepped onto a moving sidewalk. Nearby, Tory was walking alone on a deserted road. The battle had brought back all kinds of scary memories. He was more afraid of Pokémon than ever.

Tory turned and headed to a park. As he stepped onto the path, a tiny Pokémon popped up from behind a bush.

"Uh . . . later!" Tory said, stepping back. He knew the Pokémon was Plusle, an Electric Pokémon. It looked kind of like Pikachu, but with long red ears, and plus signs on its round, red cheeks. Its tail was shaped like a plus sign, too.

Plusle pulled Tory by the hand. Tory shook himself free.

"Plusle! Plusle!" the Pokémon said. It sounded upset.

Plusle pointed toward a metal garbage can. Tory heard a faint cry from within.

"*Plusle! Plusle!*" the little Plusle wanted Tory to help him.

Tory didn't know what to do. He didn't want to go near any Pokémon right now. But the little Plusle was kind of cute. And if its friend needed help . . .

Tory slowly stepped toward the garbage can.

"*Minun! Minun!*" A weak cry came from inside.

So a Minun was trapped in there. Tory knew that Minun, with its blue ears and cheeks, often paired up with Plusle. There must be one trapped inside the can.

Tory took another step closer. He reached for the lid and quickly opened it. Minun dove out. Then it jumped up, trying to hug Tory.

Tory turned and ran away—and found himself face-to-face with another Pokémon.

Tory had never seen this one before. It had a round, blue body, and stood about two feet high. It had pointy ears, big round eyes, and a wide mouth. A very wide mouth. For all Tory knew, it was highly dangerous.

"Aaaaah!" Tory screamed. Then he ran away.

Munchlax, the strange blue Pokémon, watched Tory in puzzlement. Then it shrugged and began to clean up the spilled garbage. Plusle and Minun looked at each other, then ran after Tory.

Ash and Pikachu saw the whole thing. They followed Tory to a large laboratory. He disappeared inside. Ash and Pikachu stood by the entrance. They had lost him.

Then Plusle and Minun popped up in front of Ash.

"Plusle!"

"Minun!"

They pointed down a hallway, and motioned for Ash and Pikachu to follow them. They wound through a maze of hallways until they reached an indoor garden. Rooms of green plants grew under bright lights. Plusle and Minun stopped in front of a room filled with boldly colored flowers. Ash and Pikachu stood by the doorway, silently watching.

Tory climbed into a flower bed and lay down on his back. He stared at the ceiling. Then he softly called out, "Hey, come on out!"

Nothing happened. Tory stood up. "I want to tell you something important," Tory said.

Who is he talking to? Ash wondered. But he decided to wait and see. He didn't want to scare away Tory.

Suddenly, a mysterious sound filled the garden, almost like music. In the next instant, a cluster of bright light particles appeared in front of Tory. They began to move and swirl in time to the sound.

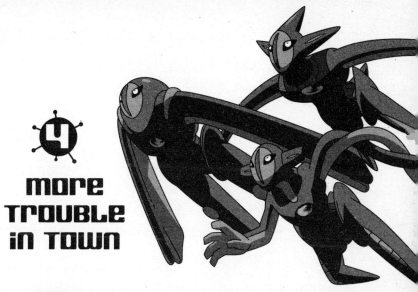

4
MORE
TROUBLE
IN TOWN

Ash and his friends weren't the only visitors to Larousse City that day. Jessie, James, and Meowth, the trio of Pokémon thieves known as Team Rocket, were entering the town, too. But they didn't arrive by monorail. They snuck up to the town's shores in a submarine shaped like a Magikarp.

Jessie, James, and Meowth climbed out of the submarine and walked down the busy Larousse City wharf. The smell of hot food drifted from the food stands lined up along the wharf.

James sniffed the air and groaned. "I'm so

hungry! How can we steal Pokémon on an empty stomach?"

Jessie, James, and Meowth made a dash for a robot selling hamburgers. "Hamburgers please!"

"Passport. Passport. Passport," the robot said, pointing to a slot on its body.

"What's a passport?" Meowth protested.

James stepped up. "Well I have no idea what kind of pass he's talking about but Meowth stop calling me sport," he said.

"HAM-BURGER!" Jessie wailed. Her long, violet-red hair streamed behind her like an angry flame. She jumped on the robot, her green eyes blazing.

"CHEESE-BURGER!" joined in Meowth. "Now! Now! Now!"

Under attack, the robot called out for help, "ALERT! ALERT! ALERT!"

But Team Rocket only fought back harder and shouted louder. Until the robot shot back with a slap against Meowth.

"That was rude!" snipped Jessie about to strike back.

"Maybe *he* takes our orders," suggested James, pointing to a second, much larger robot.

"Yeah, well I'm pretty good at giving orders so I'm going to have five hamburgers well-done," demanded Jessie. "And don't forget the French fries!"

"Well-done it is!" blared back the second robot, shooting electric blasts directly at Jessie and sending her flying.

"Jessie got fried," teased James, as Team Rocket quickly ran off.

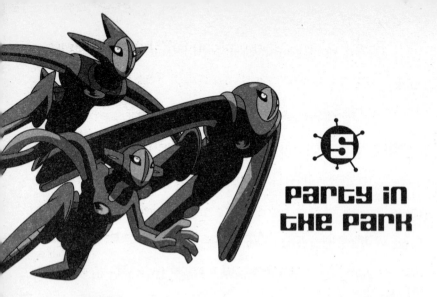

PARTY IN THE PARK

Back in the indoor garden, Ash and Pikachu watched, hidden, as Tory talked to the twinkling lights.

"You'll never guess what I just did," began Tory excitedly. "I helped out a Pokémon. It had its head stuck inside a garbage can and so I helped to get it out. Isn't that cool? And I was even part of a Pokémon battle, too! Of course I wasn't very good so that part kind of stunk . . ."

The light particles began to change, forming into various shapes and changing colors every second. Ash's curiosity got the best of him.

"Hey! Who are you talking to?" he asked Tory.

Tory turned around, startled. The light particles quickly vanished.

"Come on. Who was it?" Ash repeated.

"None of your business," Tory said crossly.

"Why would it hurt to tell me?" Ash asked.

Tory felt angry. Who was this boy in the baseball cap, anyway? So far, he had ruined everything today.

"Stop! Leave me alone. OK?" Tory yelled. Then he ran out the door.

Ash and Pikachu followed Tory out of the lab. Tory walked quickly down the sidewalk. He didn't want to talk to Ash.

"Wait a minute! I think we should battle together again," Ash said. "Bet we'll get it right next time."

"Why do you keep following me?" Tory replied. Then he stopped, his shoulders slumped.

Ash felt bad for Tory. "Are you okay?" he asked.

Tory pushed Ash away. Now it was Ash's turn to

be angry. "Why did you have to go and push me?" He grabbed Tory by his shirt.

Just in time, Brock, Max, and May came running up. May stepped between Ash and Tory.

"Ash stop!" she cried.

Tory turned his back to them. Brock frowned. He thought for a minute.

"Hey I know," he said. "Everybody follow me."

Brock led everyone to a nearby park, where he prepared a feast for his friends. The older boy had grown up taking care of his ten brothers and sisters, and he still loved to cook and clean for everyone around him. He especially loved to make special food for Pokémon.

Brock laid out the food on a picnic table. There were sandwiches and soup for all of his friends, and a plate of Pokémon food for Pikachu. Ash, Max, and May started to eat right away, but Tory was still sullen.

"There's nothing that can stop an argument better than a bunch of full mouths," Brock said.

"Try some, Tory. It's really good," suggested Ash.

Tory reluctantly took a slurp of soup. Then he smiled.

"You're right," he said.

"Told you so!" Ash replied.

The wild Pokémon in the park gathered around, attracted by the smell of Brock's cooking. A Zigzagoon stuck its head out of a hole in a tree. The furry Pokémon looked like it had a mask around its eyes. Wurmple, a little red Bug Pokémon, crawled toward the picnic table. Xatu, a colorful Psychic/Flying Pokémon, perched on a nearby tree branch. Shroomish, a Grass Pokémon that looked like a mushroom, sniffed the air along with Seedot, an acorn-shaped Grass Pokémon. And a blue and purple Zubat swooped down from the sky and flapped its wings, hovering in the air.

Brock smiled at the wild Pokémon. "There's plenty of Pokémon food, so don't be shy . . . dig in, guys," he said. Then he laid out trays of Pokémon food on the ground in front of them all. The Pokémon approached and then began to eat happily.

Tory stared at the Pokémon, nervous and fascinated at the same time.

"Tory, don't you think they are the cutest?" May asked.

"Yeah," Tory said cautiously.

"I bet they'd let you pet them," Ash suggested.

"Pikachu!" Pikachu slowly reached its hand toward Tory. Tory dropped his spoon on the table.

"Thanks guys. I'm sorry," he said. Then he got up from the table and walked off.

Ash and his friends got up from the table and watched Tory go. Ash sighed. He seemed to be doing everything wrong.

"Well, we tried," Ash said to his friends.

"I'm sure we'll get through to him eventually," added Brock.

Suddenly, Ash saw a blue Pokémon sneaking away. It was Munchlax. He was eating a sandwich.

Ash, Max, and May spun around. All of the food on the table had vanished.

"Hey you, that was our lunch!" May wailed as they chased after Munchlax.

6

An Aurora in Larousse City?

Deoxys swiftly flew through the air toward Larousse City. When it arrived, it landed on top of the Battle Tower.

There were so many life forms in Larousse City . . . how would it find the one it was looking for? Deoxys had to send out a signal.

Deoxys unleashed a blast of energy. Colorful, swirling lights began to pulse from Deoxys, growing larger and larger. Soon they filled the sky, forming a beautiful aurora.

Down below, Ash and his friends were still chasing after the Munchlax. Max saw the lights first.

"There's that light in the sky again!" Max cried.

May looked. It was like nothing she had ever seen before. "It's beautiful," she breathed.

Rafe, Sid, Audrey, and Kathryn walked up to them. Rebecca was behind them, holding up the digital camera built into her computer notebook. She began to snap pictures of the aurora.

Rebecca lowered her camera and shook her head. "But that's impossible," she said. "That's called an aurora, but it can only be seen at the North and South Poles."

"Well, then I guess we're lucky to be able to see it here, right?" May said.

Sid sidled up next to May. "The same kind of luck that brought you and me together, right babe?"

May grimaced. "Not sure what kind of luck that was!"

Brock appeared next to Rebecca. "Hi beautiful. If you're looking for a real phenomenon, stop looking in your computer and spend some time with me," he said sweetly.

Max rolled his eyes. He grabbed Brock by the collar and dragged him off. "You leaving her alone, that's a phenomenon," he muttered.

Rafe laughed. He turned to Ash. "Well, look who's still in town."

"So?" Ash replied.

"Well after that devastating defeat in front of thousands of people I thought you might be a little embarrassed to show your face," Rafe replied.

Ash felt his face growing hot. "Oh yeah, how about a rematch tomorrow in the Battle Tower?!" he challenged, glaring at Rafe.

Rafe glared back. "No problem! I'll beat you anytime and anywhere."

Rafe's confidence infuriated Ash. "I wouldn't count on that!"

Ash stopped. To his surprise, he saw Tory standing in front of him. He shyly held out a basket.

"Hey you guys! Yuko and I made these cookies for you," he said.

Ash looked inside. They had baked cookies shaped like Pokémon. Ash smiled.

"Cool Pokémon cookies," cheered Max.

Deoxys' aurora continued to shine above Larousse City. The aurora could be seen for miles away.

The aurora caught the attention of one Pokémon. Rayquaza saw the lights, and something clicked inside its brain. It remembered the Pokémon that had invaded its territory years ago . . . the Pokémon it had battled—and beaten.

And now it was back. Rayquaza roared, its cry of rage reverberating through the icy mountains.

It flew toward Larousse City with incredible speed.

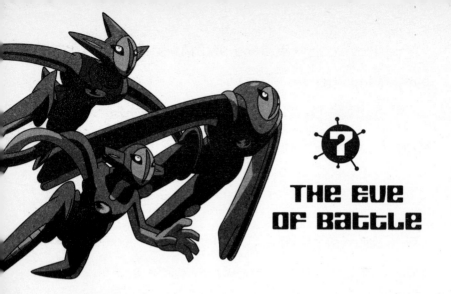

THE EVE
OF BATTLE

"**C**ome on out everyone!" called Ash. Everyone went out to the garden outside the Pokémon Center. All of the trainers released their Pokémon. Audrey and Kathryn had a Masquerain, a Bug/Flying Pokémon, and Surskit, a Bug/Water Pokémon. The cute Pokémon flew around the little girls.

Rafe's Blaziken burst from its Poké Ball.

Ash sent out Torkoal, along with three other Pokémon. Swellow flew out, flapping its dark wings. Then came Grovyle, a Grass Pokémon. Finally Corphish skittered out, clicking its claws.

May's Beautifly flew out, followed by Skitty, which looked like a cute little kitten. Bulbasaur, a Grass Pokémon with a bulb on its back, walked around the garden, sniffing the flowers. Combusken, May's Fire/Fighting Pokémon, stayed close to her side.

Brock released his Pokémon. Lombre, a Grass Pokémon, came out, smiling. Foretress, an unusual-looking Bug/Steel Pokémon, bounced out. And Mudkip, Brock's little Water Pokémon, came out and ran up to Max. They got on the swings in the garden and began to play.

"*Pika! Pika!*" Pikachu led Ash to the slide, and they raced up the ladder and slid down together.

Audrey and Kathryn started turning a jump rope. Corphish tried to jump over the rope and got tangled up. The girls laughed.

Ash noticed that Tory was standing to the side, all by himself. He walked over and stood next to Tory.

"Why don't you come play with us?" Ash asked.

"I'm fine here," Tory said, but he didn't sound fine.

Ash grabbed Tory's arm. "Come on," he urged. "It's okay."

Ash and Tory took over the jump rope. They swung it while Pokémon took turns jumping over it. Tory looked nervous at first, but soon he started to smile.

Team Rocket watched from the bushes.

"When is a sandwich more than a sandwich?" asked James.

"When the sandwich is a meal for Team Rocket to steal," Meowth said.

Jessie, James, and Meowth snuck out from behind the bushes. They tiptoed to the table. But all of the cookies were gone!

Munchlax walked away from the table, carrying a tablecloth over his shoulder. It looked like the tablecloth was full of food.

"It's stealing the food we were stealing!" Meowth complained.

"Oh no it's not!" yelled Jessie as Team Rocket ran after Munchlax.

Ash and his friends were too busy playing with their Pokémon to notice. Soon they all headed back into the Pokémon Center. Ash, Pikachu, and Tory stood on the balcony, looking out at the aurora.

"You know I've never done that before," Tory admitted.

"What," asked Ash.

Tory's eyes welled up with tears. "Just playing together with a big bunch of friends," he said. "I guess because I've always been so afraid of Pokémon. So I'm afraid to get close to Pokémon Trainers, too. Guess I've missed out on a lot."

Ash understood. "But that's all in the past," Ash said.

Pikachu looked up at Tory and smiled. Tory slowly reached a hand out toward Pikachu.

Just then, Corphish ran up. The crablike Pokémon crawled between Tory and Pikachu, waving its claws.

Tory jumped back in surprise. His hand was shaking. Ash saw how afraid he was.

"It's okay," he said. "There's no rush."

Ash glared at Corphish. They were so close! They would just have to try again in the morning.

Tory stayed overnight at the Pokémon Center. He woke up early in the morning, eager to share something with his new friends. "Come on guys, there's someone I want you to meet," he said.

"Where are we going?" Audrey asked.

"Wherever it is I hope there's a kitchen. I'm starving," added Sid, laughing.

Tory led them to the indoor garden of his father's laboratory. A security robot shaped like a Poochyena stopped in front of Tory. Tory took out an ID card, and the robot scanned it. Then it moved away.

He used his passport to open the door to the garden. The others followed him inside. They looked around at the colorful flowers in wonder.

Tory stepped into the middle of the garden. "Come on out," he called. "I'm with new my friends. Come and meet them."

Particles of light appeared in front of Tory. They formed a shape that looked something like a crystal. The lights glowed and twinkled, constantly changing colors. Everyone stared at the lights in awe.

"So this your friend, Tory?" Ash asked.

Tory nodded.

"It's gorgeous!" May said.

Rebecca began taking pictures. The lights jumped and danced around Tory, almost as though they were happy.

"Yesterday I played with all these guys and their Pokémon, too," Tory said.

The lights changed color. It looked like they were replying to Tory in some way.

"Wow, that's so cool Tory," Audrey remarked.

Tory nodded. "And it even understands what I say!"

"Is it a Pokémon?" May asked.

"Not one that I've ever seen," added Max.

The light flew around Rafe, Audrey, Kathryn, and Sid. It almost seemed like it was studying them.

"What do you say I introduce my Pokémon to it?" Rafe asked. He threw out a Poké Ball, and Blaziken emerged.

Sid released his Blastoise, and Rebecca released Metagross, a Steel/Psychic Pokémon with four sturdy legs attached to its round body.

"Don't forget ours!" said Audrey and Kathryn. They released Surskit and Masquerain.

The light particles happily danced around the Pokémon. Tory smiled.

Officer Jenny's monitor showed the air space

over Larousse City. Rayquaza was speeding toward the town. She quickly put in a call to Professor Lund.

"How could a Rayquaza be coming here?" she asked him.

"I don't know but for it to leave the ozone layer again there must be a powerful reason," Lund replied.

"Do you see that?" Yuko asked. She magnified another image on her computer screen. Yuko stared at the image, stunned.

"It's Deoxys!" he cried. "Rayquaza must have come here after sensing that Deoxys was here as well. If those two battle it out in our city, the result will be catastrophic! Evacuate Larousse City immediately!"

"Right away, sir!" Officer Jenny replied. "Initializing emergency evacuation!"

Immediately, alarms began ringing through the town followed by Officer Jenny's emergency message, "Fellow citizens, we are facing an emergency situation. Please evacuate immediately!"

8

EVACUATE!

The alarms did not bother Deoxys. It flew back and forth over Larousse City, searching . . . searching.

There were too many life forms. Too much electromagnetic energy. Deoxys landed in the center of town. It launched another Psycho Boost.

All of the machines hit by the blast stopped working. Even the robots lost power.

That was better. Thing were quieter now. Deoxys released another aurora into the sky. Maybe its signal would be seen now. . . .

Back at the lab, Professor Lund raced outside. Yuko followed him.

"Tory's out in the garden," he said.

"I have to go out and get him," Lund said. "Everyone, evacuate immediately!"

Lund raced down the moving sidewalk. It was crowded with people trying to escape the town. Yuko watched him go. She wasn't going to evacuate the town—not if it meant leaving Lund and Tory behind. Besides, somebody had to try to find out what was happening with Rayquaza and Deoxys.

Lund ran against the crowd on the sidewalk, frantically searching for Tory. Suddenly, the sidewalk stopped. A computer voice rang out.

"Losing power. All systems will now shut down."

People didn't stop. They ran down the sidewalk, toward the river. Lund got pulled along with the crowd.

Down at the wharf, the block-shaped security robots had joined together to form a bridge over the river. With the monorail shut down, the bridge was the only way out of town.

Jessie, James, and Meowth pushed their way through the crowd.

"Some vacation this turned out to be," Meowth said.

"Whose bad idea was this?" asked Jessie.

"Let's just say Meowth and I were overruled," replied James.

Team Rocket looked up. Deoxys flew overhead.

Suddenly, something strange happened. Two more Deoxys emerged from Deoxys's body. They looked like shadows of the real thing.

Each Deoxys Shadow split into two more Deoxys Shadows. They kept splitting and splitting, until dozens of Deoxys Shadows crowded the sky. The people on the ground screamed in terror.

All at once, the Deoxys Shadows swooped down from the sky. They began scooping up people and flying off with them. One Deoxys Shadow zoomed down and grabbed Jessie, James, and Meowth.

"Hey!" Meowth wailed.

Lund stood, stunned, as the Deoxys Shadows kept coming. Officer Jenny ran up to him and grabbed him by the wrist.

"Professor, you must escape!" she insisted.

"Let go of me!" Lund cried.

The professor struggled, but Officer Jenny pulled him onto the bridge.

Flying over the wharf, Deoxys paused. It sensed something. An old enemy.

Deoxys unleashed a powerful Aurora Beam. Golden light poured from its body, spreading wider and wider until a bubble of light encased the entire island.

Rayquaza zoomed toward the barrier. Then it crashed into the light and let out a scream. An intense blast of electricity sent Rayquaza reeling backward.

Professor Lund watched helplessly from the robot bridge. The bubble separated them from the town, now. There had to be some way to get back. He tried to run across the bridge.

But the electric blast fried the security robots that formed the bridge. The robots began to fall apart, and the bridge started to crumble. There was nothing Lund could do but run back to the other side, to safety.

Inside the bubble, he could still see the Deoxys Shadows flying, capturing everyone in their path. What would happen to the people left behind?

"Tory!" Professor Lund wailed.

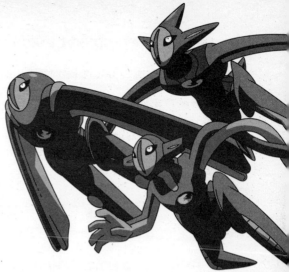

9
RACE TO SAFETY

Down in the indoor garden, Ash and the others heard the alarms ring out. The automatic door to the garden began to open and shut repeatedly.

"What's that?" asked Ash.

"It sounds like the police," answered Rafe.

Tory inserted his ID card, but the door wouldn't stop.

"Why won't your passport work?" Ash asked.

"This never happens!" Tory replied sounding a bit worried.

Sid stepped up and tried to hold the door open with both hands. But it kept closing anyway.

Then a buzzer rang out.

The light particles vanished. Tory cried out in dismay.

At the same time, the door stopped moving. It was stuck in a half-open, half-closed position.

The friends pushed and pushed until they forced the door open. They ran out through the door and into the hallway.

Deoxys appeared directly in front of them.

"What is that thing?" Ash asked.

"Deoxys!" cried out Tory. He remembered seeing this Pokémon years ago, on the ice field.

"You know its name?" Rafe asked, surprised.

Before their eyes, two Deoxys Shadows emerged from Deoxys. Then each of those split into two more Deoxys Shadows. The terrifying Pokémon surrounded the children.

One of the Deoxys Shadows dived at Sid. The boy jumped out of the way.

"Blastoise, Hydro Pump!" Sid yelled.

Blastoise fired its water cannons at the Deoxys Shadow. The blast of water hit the Pokémon directly in its center. The Deoxys Shadow vanished.

But another Deoxys Shadow swept up behind Sid. It grabbed the boy and his Blastoise. Sid screamed as the Pokémon carried them away.

"Sid!" Rafe yelled. He turned to Blaziken. "Blaziken, Flamethrower!"

"Pikachu, Thunderbolt!" Ash cried.

The Pokémon attacked at once. Blaziken swiped at the Deoxys Shadows with a flaming fist. Pikachu launched a powerful jolt of electricity.

The Deoxys Shadows pulled back from the attackers.

"Tory, is there another way out?" Rebecca asked.

Tory led them to an emergency exit. He opened

the door, and they followed him outside into an alleyway outside the lab. Yuko came limping down the alley.

"There you are!" Yuko called.

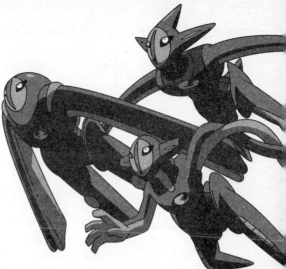

10

A FiGHt FOr SurViVaL

The Deoxys Shadows swarmed around Larousse City like bees. Deoxys flew above them, sending them commands with its mind.

One by one, the Deoxys Shadows scooped up every person and Pokémon they could find. Then they carried them all to a large stadium on the edge of the island. The stadium was shaped like a golf ball.

Meanwhile, Yuko led Ash, his friends, and their Pokémon to Professor Lund's lab. Yuko looked around at the fried computers. "The entire town is enclosed within a force field, making it impossible to come in or leave," she explained. "Communication with the outside has been cut off, too."

"Hey Tory? What did you call that thing? Was it Deoxys?" asked Ash.

"That's right," Yuko said. "It's a Pokémon from outer space."

"What?" Ash couldn't believe it.

Yuko told the story of Deoxys. "Four years ago, a meteorite struck the North Pole," she began. "And located inside of it was a completely unknown Pokémon. Professor Lund named it Deoxys."

"But almost immediately Rayquaza appeared and attacked Deoxys. Rayquaza was threatened and thought Deoxys was invading its territory. Deoxys vanished . . . deep into the sea."

"So I don't get it. How can that be the same Deoxys?" Brock asked.

Yuko looked thoughtful. "It must have been regenerating."

"Regenerating?" Rebecca asked. She began typing in her notebook.

"Deoxys has astounding regenerative powers," Yuko explained. "Professor Lund and I have been studying this all these years."

Audrey and Kathryn were shivering.

"I'm so hungry," said one little girl.

"So am I," said the other.

Ash, Tory, Brock, Rafe, and Rebecca all decided to go in search of food and water. Ash had Pikachu with him, and Rafe and Rebecca had Blaziken and Metagross. When they stepped outside, they surveyed the area. Deoxys Shadows flew across the sky in the distance.

While Rebecca and Rafe went to find out where all the people had been taken. Ash, Tory, and Brock went to find food and water.

A few blocks away, Ash discovered a robot food vendor. It had a picture of a hot dog on the sign on the front. Ash inserted his passport, but no food came out.

"Still no good," Tory said. "Nothing's happening."

"I can see the food in there," Ash said. "We just need to figure out a way to break in."

"Pika!" Pikachu said. Ash and Brock stepped back.

Zap! Pikachu charged the robot with an electric blast. Hot dogs began to shoot out of the machine.

"Whoa! Gotta catch them all!" Brock said. He scooped them up in his arms.

"Sssssh!" Ash said, pointing.

A Deoxys Shadow had landed on a nearby building. They quickly hid behind the food stand. The Deoxys Shadow flew toward the stand. They held their breath.

Plusle and Minun jumped in front of them and blasted the Deoxys Shadow with Electric Attacks.

The Pokémon dodged the attacks. It reached down and grabbed Minun. It started to fly away.

IN THE FROZEN NORTH, A METEOR FALLS FROM THE SKY.

A STRANGE POKEMON EMERGES.

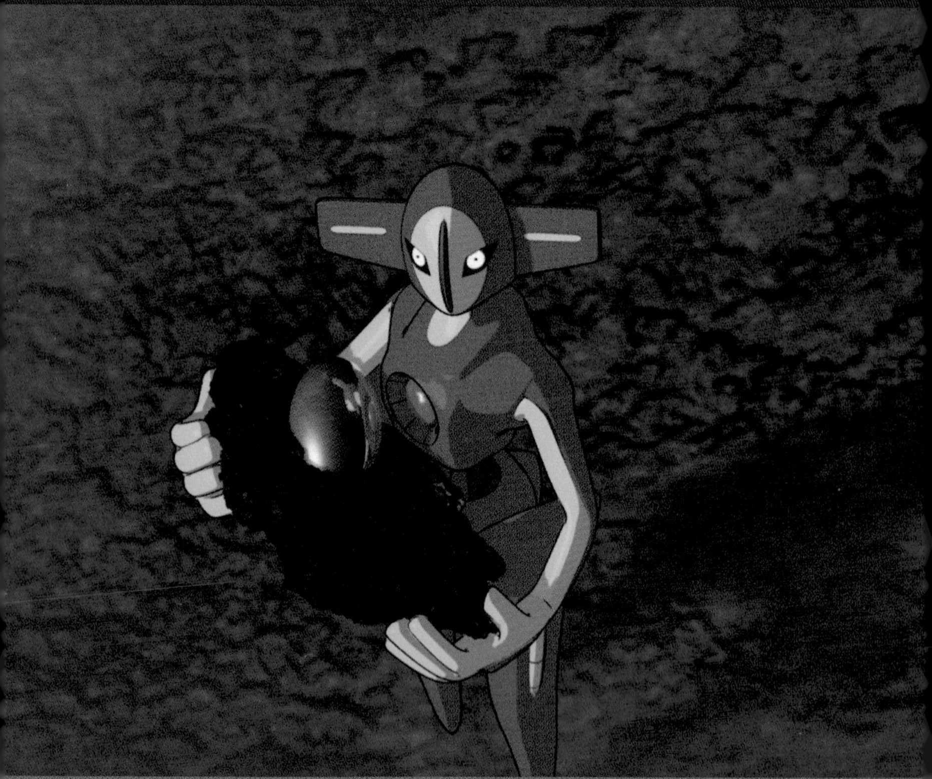

RAYQUAZA IS ON THE ATTACK!

TORY WITNESSES
THE ENTIRE BATTLE!

FOUR YEARS LATER . . .
ASH AND HIS FRIENDS TRAVEL
TO LAROUSSE CITY.

LAROUSSE CITY IS HOME
TO TRAINERS LIKE SID
AND REBECCA.

LAROUSSE CITY IS ALSO
HOME TO POKÉMON LIKE
PLUSLE AND MINUN.

ASH AND PIKACHU ARE READY
TO TAKE ON THE CHALLENGE
OF HELPING TORY
OVERCOME HIS FEARS.

Ash charged toward Minun, but in the next instant, another Deoxys Shadow zoomed in and grabbed Tory. Ash jumped up and grabbed the Deoxys Shadow by the arm. Brock grabbed another arm. The Deoxys Shadow couldn't fly away.

"Pikachu, Thunderbolt!"

A yellow lightning bolt zapped the Deoxys Shadow. With a scream, the Pokémon released Tory.

Ash knew more Deoxys Shadows were probably on the way. He scooped up Plusle in one arm and grabbed Tory's hand with the other. Then he ran.

"But Minun!" Tory protested.

"Plusle! Plusle!" Plusle whined.

"Sorry," Ash said gruffly. "It's too late."

Ash turned the corner. The street was a row of storage rooms. Ash ducked into one of the rooms with Tory and Plusle, and Brock and Pikachu followed. They hid behind some old crates.

Ash peeked out to see the Deoxys walk past. Then it moved on.

"That was close," Ash whispered.

Plusle began to cry. Tory felt terrible.

"It was all my fault . . .," his voice trailed off. He reached out a hand. He wanted to pet Plusle, to make it feel better. But he still couldn't do it.

"I should have . . .," Tory said sadly.

"Pikachu!" Pikachu cried out. It pointed to one of the crates.

Brock looked inside. "Look what I just found. Precious water!" he said.

"All right!" Ash said.

11
A DARING
PLAN

When Ash, Brock, Tory, Pikachu, and Plusle got back to the lab, they found that Rafe and Rebecca had already returned. With a little help from Yuko, they discovered the Deoxys had been carting the people away to the stadium.

That very moment, a loud crash shook the lab. Audrey and Kathryn shrieked with alarm.

Bam! Bam! Bam! Something kept slamming into the office door.

"Let's get out of here!" Rebecca cried.

Yuko nodded. "Yes, there's a secret underground lab. Let's go!" She limped to an emergency door across the room and pressed a button. The door opened to reveal a staircase leading downward.

"Try and stay calm! Go!" Yuko said reassuringly.

The twins went first, followed by their Pokémon. Then came Max, May, Plusle, and Munchlax. The staircase led to a ladder that led straight down. Ash and Pikachu climbed down and found themselves in a huge lab filled with blinking lights and computers.

"What is this place?" Ash asked.

In the center of the lab was a glass room. Inside the room were several machines surrounding a plexiglass case that held what looked like a crystal egg.

"The lab where we studied Deoxys, and its regeneration," Yuko said. "There were actually two of them before. Rayquaza defeated one while the other Deoxys was dormant inside of this meteorite."

Everyone was stunned.

"That crystal is a part of Deoxys," Yuko explained.

Tory stared at the crystal, fascinated. Slowly, particles of light appeared in front of Tory's face and began to dance.

Now it was Yuko's turn to be stunned.

"Hey, Tory it's your friend!" Ash said.

"Wait a second," said May. "Then Tory's friend is . . ."

"Right!" interrupted Rebecca. "It's Deoxys!"

The lights began to dance and change color. As Rebecca watched the lights, her eyes suddenly lit up.

"That's it," she said. "It all makes sense!"

Rebecca flipped open her notebook. She tapped some keys, and a picture of the aurora came up.

"This is Tory's friend's light pattern and this is the pattern of the aurora that covered Larousse!" she said. "I think it might be how they communicate."

"So can you tell what it's saying?" May asked.

Rebecca pointed to the screen. "This one means 'friend,'" she explained. "And this one seems to be asking, 'Where are you?'"

Everyone turned to the crystal.

"So it's just looking for its friend?" Ash asked.

The lights changed color.

"Of course!" Yuko said. "Deoxys carried off all those people and Pokémon because they were interfering while it searched for its friend."

"What?" Audrey asked.

"Deoxys sees certain types of electrical fields," Yuko said. "That's probably why Deoxys shut down all the robots. But it's not just electrical devices, humans and Pokémon emit them, too. They were blocking its vision."

A look of understanding crossed Rafe's face. "So that's why its moving them out of the way," Rafe said.

"Please, Yuko," pleaded Tory. "You've got to help this Deoxys regenerate."

Tory looked at the crystal. "It's so sad. It's been alone all of this time."

The lights danced in front of Tory's face.

Ash guessed. "Once Deoxys finds its friend, it will go back home."

"But we need more electricity," Yuko admitted. "The backup generator that's keeping the lab working now isn't powerful enough to operate the device."

"If it's electricity you want, then I'm your guy," Rafe said.

"I can get the wind generators going," Rebecca said.

Ash remembered the windmills lining the shore of the island.

"Can we help?" asked Audrey and Kathryn.

"Yes, we'll need everyone's help to save those people and Pokémon. Let's start working on a plan and then we'll go out to where they're being held!" Rafe said.

Rebecca pressed a button on her notebook. A photo of the sports dome appeared.

"I'll zero in on it," Rebecca said.

Ash hated to admit it, but Rafe had a pretty good plan. "Let's go get them!" Ash cried.

Everyone slowly walked back up to Professor Lund's office. Thankfully, the Deoxys Shadows had given up trying to break down the door and were nowhere in sight.

They walked outside to a moving sidewalk that wasn't moving anymore. The streets of Larousse City were deserted. There were no people or Pokémon in sight—and no Deoxys Shadows, either.

Then, without warning, Deoxys appeared in front of them. Ash realized this wasn't a shadow, but the real thing.

"Deoxys! We're not your enemies. We're your friends," called Ash. "If you'll just trust us we can help you find your friend. I promise."

Deoxys moved in. An electromagnetic wave shot from its body, zapping them all as dozens of Deoxys Shadows appeared.

"Blaziken!" Rafe shouted.

"Pikachu, Thunderbolt!" Ash cried.

"Pikachuuuuuuuu!" Pikachu hurled a sizzling

Thunderbolt at the Deoxys Shadow closest to Audrey. Stunned by the blow, it stepped back. Blaziken quickly grabbed the little girl.

"Quick! Now's our chance!" Rebecca yelled.

Tory led the way as they charged through the building. Rafe and Blaziken brought up the rear. A Deoxys Shadow flew toward them, and Rafe stopped.

"Blaziken, Overheat!" he yelled.

Blaziken pounded the Deoxys Shadow. Ash stopped.

"Go ahead, Ash!" Rafe cried. "Just don't let anything happen to my sisters!"

"You can count on that," Ash called back. There was nothing else he could do now.

Tory led them up a staircase and back to the street. Ash didn't look behind. But he heard Blaziken cry out, and then a shout from Rafe.

The Deoxys Shadows had got them. Ash knew it. But he couldn't stop now. They had to put their plan into action, or this would never end.

The group ran along a moving sidewalk. The sports dome rose up in the distance. They didn't have far to go. . . .

Suddenly, a huge, green Pokémon swooped down through the sky. Its long body looked like a tornado hurling through space. Rayquaza had broken through the barrier!

12

DEOXYS B

Several Deoxys Shadows immediately appeared and surrounded Rayquaza. The fierce Pokémon blasted them with Hyper Beam. The powerful blast of energy tore through the Deoxys Shadows, and many of them vaporized on contact.

Rayquaza didn't stop. It kept blasting the Deoxys Shadows with one Hyper Beam after another. Deoxys flew up to face Rayquaza.

Ash saw their chance to escape. "All right, let's do this like we planned!"

Brock grabbed Audrey and Kathryn. They ran off with Rebecca, Max, and May toward the wind generation plant. Surskit and Masquerain flew behind them.

Ash, Pikachu, Tory, Plusle, and Munchlax ran off toward the sports dome. They quickly reached the entrance.

"Rafe, Sid, we came to help you!" Ash yelled.

Inside, Rafe, Sid, and Minun were sitting with Jessie, James, and Meowth. Rafe jumped to his feet.

"We're up here!" Rafe said.

Ash pulled on the door. "It's locked!"

"You'll have to destroy the door's electrical lock," Rafe explained.

Pikachu nodded. It blasted the door with an electric charge. Ash tried the door again, but it wouldn't open.

"No good!" Ash called out.

James stood up. "To break an electric lock, you have to zap it from both sides of the door at once," he said.

Jessie picked up Minun and dropped it in front of the door. The little Pokémon nodded.

"Minun!" It zapped the door with an electric blast.

On the other side, Pikachu charged the door again. This time, Plusle helped, too.

The electric blasts charged the door, zapping Team Rocket. They fell to the floor. But the plan worked, and the door swung open. Minun ran to Plusle, and they hugged.

"Where are my sisters?" Rafe asked.

"They're on the way to the wind generator," Ash said.

"Rayquaza!"

The Dragon/Flying Pokémon swooped toward the stadium in pursuit of a Deoxys Shadow. A glowing Hyper Beam shot from Rayquaza's mouth, destroying it instantly.

The light beam also blasted the stadium, and

debris showered down in front of the entrance. There was no time to run out of the way.

But they didn't have to. Deoxys swept in and blasted the rubble, vaporizing it before it could fall on them. Then Deoxys flew up and faced Rayquaza directly.

"We've got to get out of here!" Ash said urgently.

Jessie, James, and Meowth staggered to their feet. "Don't leave us!" Jessie begged.

"We're coming with you!" James cried.

They all ran through the sports dome, freeing the people and Pokémon inside. Then they headed back to the streets. Above them, Rayquaza and Deoxys traded attacks in the sky.

Rayquaza unleashed a Hyper Beam. Deoxys transformed, sending the Hyper Beam flying back.

Rayquaza didn't give up. It zipped toward Deoxys, quickly moving back and forth. Then it wrapped its snakelike body around Deoxys, constricting tightly.

Ash hoped Deoxys would be all right. The best thing he could do was help to bring Deoxys B back to life. But they had to hurry.

"Sid and I will take everyone to the generator," Rafe said. "You guys get back to the lab. Hurry!"

Ash knew they had to move fast. On the ground, he saw a broken piece of robot with wheels on the bottom. He jumped on.

"Tory, Pikachu, get on!"

Tory and Pikachu jumped on board. Plusle and Minun jumped up and grabbed Ash. Ash realized that Munchlax was nowhere in sight. But he couldn't worry about that now. He had to help Deoxys.

Thanks to the makeshift skateboard, they quickly reached the underground lab. Yuko was waiting for them.

"Everything is ready," she said.

Down at the power plant, Brock had everyone working together to get the windmills moving. Some people and Pokémon were pulling on ropes to get the turbines going. Other Pokémon were using their moves to make the turbines spin.

Jessie, James, and Meowth jumped on bicycles hooked up to the turbines. They began to pedal furiously.

Slowly, the windmills began to turn. The harder everyone worked, the faster they turned.

In the sky above them, Rayquaza still held Deoxys in its grip. Then Deoxys released an Aurora Beam from its body. The force sent Rayquaza flying, and Deoxys was free. It faced Rayquaza again.

Down in the underground lab, the electricity came back on.

"We've got power back," Yuko said. "We can start regeneration!"

Yuko typed in a security code and entered the glass-enclosed area that held the Deoxys B crystal. The others followed her. She pointed to the switch.

"This will start the process," she said.

"You should turn it on," Ash said. "It is your friend, after all."

Yuko nodded. Tory stepped up to the switch.

"Here goes," he said. Then he flipped it.

A laser beam shot out at the Deoxys B crystal. The crystal started to glow. But then the beam started to flicker on and off.

Yuko looked at the control board and frowned. "We're still twenty percent short on energy!"

Ash knew how to fix that. "Pikachu, Plusle, Minun, you know what to do!"

The three Pokémon quickly obeyed. They blasted the control panel with electric shocks.

The laser beam began to glow brightly. The power was so intense that steam rose up from the control machines. Soon steam filled the little room.

The plexiglass surrounding the Deoxys B crystal shattered. The steam parted to reveal Deoxys B standing there. Tory looked at the Pokémon in awe.

"Deoxys, it's really you!" he said.

Deoxys B nodded.

"Do you want to meet your friend now?" Tory asked.

A soft aurora light came from Deoxys B's body. The light enveloped Tory, Ash, and Pikachu.

Deoxys B began to fly up into the air. Ash, Tory, and Pikachu floated up next to it, still in a bubble of light.

They headed up an elevator shaft. Deoxys B crashed through the roof. Ash looked down at the town below.

They were flying!

ATTACK OF THE ROBOTS

The battle between Rayquaza and Deoxys raged on. Rayquaza wrapped its body around Deoxys again. Then it threw Deoxys onto the roof of the Battle Tower. Deoxys crashed into the roof.

The Pokémon took a lot of damage. The force field it had been sustaining over Larousse City collapsed. A strong wind swept through the town.

The wind swept through the power generation plant, sending the windmills spinning. Rafe led the people there in a cheer.

"The power is on again!" he cried.

Angry and hurt, Deoxys let out a huge roar. A giant electromagnetic wave poured out from its body. The entire Battle Tower began to charge with electricity. Machines jumped back into operation. The moving sidewalk zipped along once again.

Outside the Pokémon Center, the block-shaped security robots came back to life. Confused, they started to group together.

The blast missed Rayquaza. It flew down toward Deoxys. When it got in range, it hurled a powerful Hyper Beam.

But the beam didn't hit its target. Deoxys B swept in and deflected the attack.

Deoxys looked up and saw Deoxys B. It stood up. Deoxys B deposited Ash, Tory, and Pikachu on the rooftop. Then the two Pokémon stared at each other, and the crystal inside each one of them began to glow. A new aurora appeared in the sky above.

"They finally met," Tory said.

But the beautiful moment didn't last. Rayquaza swooped down again, launching another Hyper Beam.

The two Deoxys moved together. They repelled the Hyper Beam. Then laser beams shot from each of their crystals. The beams blasted Rayquaza, and it tumbled down from the sky, crashing into the street below.

Ash felt the roof beneath them begin to crumble. The roof was caving in.

"Pikachu!" Pikachu cried.

Ash, Pikachu, and Tory started to fall. But Deoxys B flew up and caught them. The two Deoxys flew down to the street outside the Battle Tower. They examined the fallen Rayquaza.

Rayquaza was clearly injured. It tried to stand up, but couldn't.

"We've got to help Rayquaza," Ash said. He hated to see any Pokémon get hurt.

Then Ash noticed something. A group of

security robots had surrounded them all. The robots began joining together. They formed a huge shape that looked almost like a robot that was part Deoxys, part Rayquaza.

"What's going on?" Ash wondered.

The block robots faced Rayquaza. Then, without warning, they blasted Rayquaza with a laser beam. The blast sent Rayquaza flying.

Ash knew something was wrong with the robots. They were out of control. They would probably destroy Rayquaza if somebody didn't stop them.

"Everything's totally out of control! Let's try and get back to Yuko," Ash suggested.

"Tory can you hear me? TORY?" came Professor Lund's voice over the monitor.

"Daddy?" Tory answered, turning toward the monitor.

"You must listen to me very carefully. All of the block robots are malfunctioning. We no longer have power over the robots from the booth. But the chief robot that controls all of the others should be near you. You must present your passport to the chief robot. Then everything should unlock for just enough time for us to regain control and shut down the security system! Son, the fate of our town is in your hands. I know we can count on you!"

"Don't worry sir, Pikachu and I are going to help Tory," reassured Ash. "We have to get to that tower. Quick, let's go!"

Tory and Ash raced to the Battle Tower. The chief robot was easy to pick out. It was shaped like a Poochyena and stood taller than all the block robots.

But there were so many block robots and they seemed to be multiplying. There was no stopping them. Soon the robots had Tory, Plusle, and Minun surrounded.

Now it was up to Ash alone to disarm them. He ran toward the chief robot. The blocks were right behind him. Suddenly, he ran into Munchlax.

"What are you doing here?" Ash asked.

It didn't matter. The blocks surrounded Ash, Pikachu, and Munchlax. Ash pushed against the robots. There was no way out.

Suddenly, a flash of light appeared from inside the blocks. The blast knocked back the robots, scattering them. Ash and Pikachu landed on the ground.

Another Pokémon landed next to them. But it wasn't Munchlax. It was a huge Snorlax! Ash realized what had happened.

"You evolved into Snorlax!" he said.

Snorlax yawned.

Ash looked back at the constantly growing pile of block robots. He could still see the chief robot. He had to reach it. They charged toward the chief robot. Block robots came toward them.

"Pikachu!" Pikachu blasted each one away with an electric charge.

It gave Ash the chance he needed. He jumped up and grabbed a hold of the chief robot. By now all of the blocks had joined together, and the giant robot they had formed loomed next to the Battle Tower. Suddenly, Ash dropped his passport.

"NOOOOOOO!!" he cried.

Tory tossed Ash his passport. "Use mine!" he called.

"This better work!" Ash said.

With that, Ash stuck his passport card into the slot on the chief robot. The block robots suddenly stopped moving. There was silence.

"It worked!" Tory cheered.

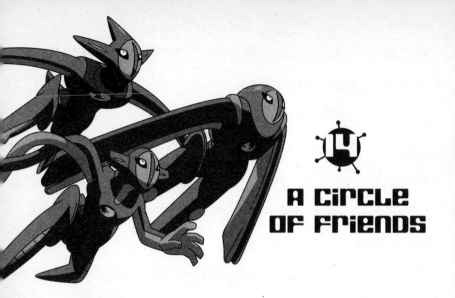

4
A CIRCLE
OF FRIENDS

Deoxys B flew in, grabbing them all just moments before they touched the ground.

An aurora shone from Deoxys B's body. Ash, Pikachu, Plusle, Minun, and Tory were suspended in the light once again.

Deoxys made an aurora, too. It rose from the fallen robots, holding Rayquaza in its arms. The two light fields joined together, sweeping over the entire town.

The light helped revive Rayquaza. It flew out of

Deoxys' arms and up into the sky, emitting a joyful cry. Then it disappeared over the horizon.

Ash felt like he was floating. The light of the aurora felt warm and safe. Reaching out, he grabbed Tory's hand. Tory, Pikachu, Plusle, and Minun joined hands, too. Deoxys and Deoxys B joined them, forming a circle.

The circle of friends floated up, swirling in the light of the aurora. Down below, Ash could see his friends smiling, bathing in the light of the aurora as well.

"Thank you, Deoxys," Tory said to his friend.

Deoxys B nodded.

Then they slowly began to descend to Earth. Ash and his friends landed on the ground. Deoxys and Deoxys B floated above them.

"Good-bye. I'll miss you," Tory said.

The two Deoxys floated up higher and higher. The aurora floated away with them.

"I wonder where they're going?" Tory asked.

"Wherever they're going, they'll always have each other," Ash said.

"Pika!" Pikachu agreed.

Then the aurora faded altogether, and the two Deoxys vanished from sight.

Pikachu jumped into Ash's arms. Rafe and Ash shook hands. Audrey and Kathryn hugged Max. Rebecca gave Brock a kiss on the cheek. Snorlax snored nearby, fast asleep.

Professor Lund and Yuko ran up. Tory hugged his father.

"I'm so happy you're safe," Lund said.

"But I'm only okay," Tory said, "because of my friends."

Plusle and Minun hugged Tory's legs. Tory hugged them back. Then he began to gently pet each one on the head. Professor Lund looked at Yuko, and they both smiled.

Back at the wind generation plant, Jessie, James, and Meowth were still pedaling their bicycles furiously.

The next day, Ash and his friends left Larousse City. They left the island on a small ferry. Tory stood on the pier to see them off with Plusle, Minun, and Snorlax.

Tory was sad to see Ash go. But he had his own Pokémon now—and he had other friends now, too. He walked away from the pier to find Rafe, Sid, Audrey, and Kathryn waiting for him. He grinned and ran toward them.

Rebecca was happy, too. She and Metagross took jobs in Professor Lund's lab, helping Yuko.

Back on the boat, Ash looked up at the sky, remembering floating there with the two Deoxys. What an incredible adventure!

And in the cold North, the two Deoxys flew

across the ice field. Their crystals glowed brightly inside them.

After years of waiting, they were reunited at last.